Where is everybody?
It's time to play.

I look in the bathroom.
Where can they be?

I think they must all
be hiding from me...

There's something
in the laundry basket
that looks very fat.

Guess what I find there?

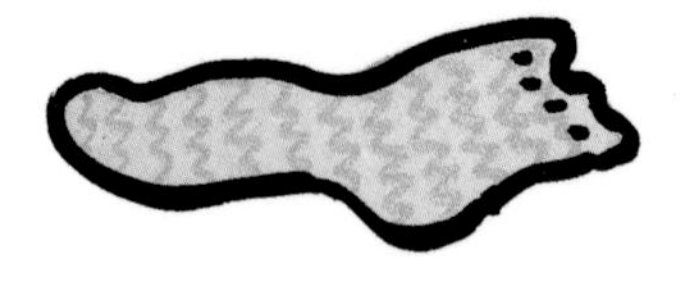

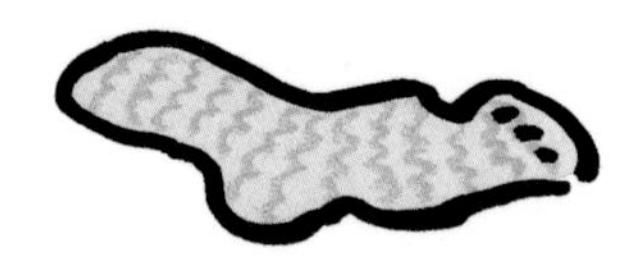

I go into the playroom
and look under the chairs.

I look behind the curtains
and under the stairs...

There's something
in the cat's bed
that looks like a log.

Guess what I find there?

CAT

I go into the kitchen
and hear a strange sound.

I look under the table
and all around...

There's something
in the dog's bed
that looks like a sheep.

Guess what I find there?

I say,
“Come on, everybody.

It's time for our trip!"

What do we ride on?

I am the captain –

and who is my crew?

Cats, dogs and brothers,

and Mum and Dad too!